A NOTE TO PARENTS

Sales is one of the greatest professions in the world, when done right. It's all around us because everything we see has to be sold in some way to get to where it is. Whether or not it's our chosen profession, we're all in sales. We sell ourselves and our ideas every day when we interview, debate with others, get funding or support for our ideas, or try to convince others to do what we want them to do, especially our kids.

Unfortunately, sales is often portrayed negatively in movies and TV shows. It is one of the most popular careers in the world, yet very few institutions offer college degrees in sales. This lack of formal education and standards can lead to poor experiences for the consumer. The good news is we can improve the reputation of the sales industry by starting early and educating ourselves on how to do it right.

Let's introduce our children to the positive side of sales right from the start. As a parent with a career in sales, it's important to me that there is a book available for children that paints this career as something children can be proud of. Who knows? Maybe one day, your child will be the first to answer that age-old question of "What do you want to do when you grow up?" with the answer "Sales!"

J. barrows

I dedicate this book to my daughter.
Charlotte, believe in yourself as much as
Mommy and Daddy believe in you, and
there is nothing you can't accomplish.

www.mascotbooks.com

I Want to Be in Sales When I Grow Up!

For more information, please contact:
Mascot Books
620 Herndon Parkway #320
Herndon, VA 20170
info@mascotbooks.com

Library of Congress Control Number: 2019900600

CPSIA Code: PRT0419A
ISBN-13: 978-1-64307-238-8

Printed in the United States

I WANT TO BE IN SALES WHEN I GROW UP!

Written by
John Barrows

Illustrated by
Juan Diaz

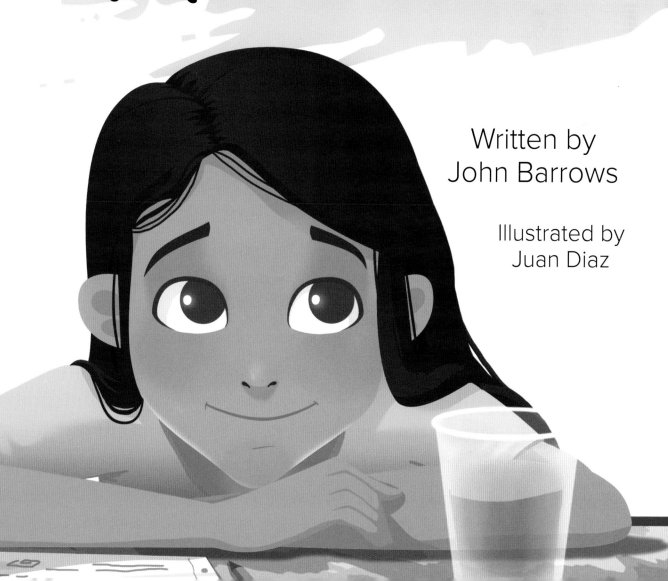

Charlie's favorite day of the whole school year was career day. She loved meeting all the grownups and learning about their jobs. There were so many different careers!

"Gather around, everyone!" said Miss Katie as career day ended. "I hope you all had a good time today. Now form a line and pick a career from the hat to write your report on."

Charlie reached her hand into the hat, hoping she'd get something cool like a firefighter.

"Sales? That's a career? How am I supposed to write a report about sales?"

Charlie got home and put her backpack down in a huff.
"Sales," she mumbled. "Why did I have to get sales?"
How was she even supposed to start?

"Sales, eh?" said her dad, peering over her shoulder. "Why are you talking about sales?"

"I have to do a report on sales for career day," said Charlie. "I don't even know what sales is. I've seen people sell things in movies and on TV, but that doesn't look like something I would want to do."

"Well, let's think about it for a minute. In reality, sales is all around us!" said Charlie's mom. "It's a very important part of everyday life. Take this butter dish for example. Someone had to make this and sell it to someone else before we could buy it at the store to hold our butter."

"Otherwise, we'd have butter all over our hands!" said Charlie's dad.

"Sales connects people to the things they need," he continued. "Look around, everything in this kitchen was sold at one point in time!"

"But what should I do for my report?" said Charlie.

"Why don't you try to sell something and then write about what you learned? Let's think about what you could sell. What do you have that people need or want?"

"All my friends like my stuffed animals," said Charlie.

"That's true, but you wouldn't want to sell them, would you?" asked Charlie's mom.

"No, you're right, I wouldn't," said Charlie. "They like the cookies I make. Could I make some of those and sell them?"

"I think that's a great idea," said her mom. "Grab your apron and let's make it happen!"

When dinner ended, Charlie grabbed her apron and got to work.

"Where are the nuts, Mom?" she asked. "I love nutty chocolate chip cookies!"

"Here you go," said her mom. "It's always important to sell what you love."

Charlie made sure to measure every ingredient perfectly and mix everything together. She even used an ice cream scoop to put the dough on the pan so the cookies would be nice and round.

Soon, the kitchen smelled of delicious, freshly baked cookies.

"I better taste one just to be sure they're okay," said Charlie.

"Good idea," said her mom. "I'll taste one too."

"People are going to love these!" said Charlie. "I can't wait to get out there and sell them!"

After they were done making the cookies, Charlie's dad asked, "So how do you plan on selling them?"

"I was just going to sell them to my classmates," said Charlie.

"That's not a bad idea," said Charlie's dad, "but do the kids at school usually have money on them?"

"Some do," said Charlie, "but they usually use it for lunch. But some kids pack their lunches!"

"Yes," said Charlie's dad, "but I bet most of them already have a cookie in them. Remember, in order to be successful in sales you need to find people who can buy what you're selling and also have a need for it."

"Hmm," said Charlie. "What if I went around the neighborhood and sold them to the parents? They're the ones who pack the lunches, right?"

"Now that's a great idea!"

The next day after school, Charlie set out with her parents and her cookies. It was time to go door to door.

Charlie knocked on the first door, heart racing. She was more nervous than she thought she would be. After a few minutes passed, an older gentleman opened the door.

"Um...hello," Charlie stammered. "I've made some cookies, um, if you want to buy some. Please."

"And who are you?" the gentleman asked.

"Oh, I'm Charlie," said Charlie. "And I made these cookies."

"You already said that," said the gentleman with a smirk. "But you didn't say how much they cost."

Charlie panicked and quickly walked away. This was going to be harder than she thought.

Charlie knocked on the next door. No one answered. She knocked again just in case.

"Let's try the next one, honey," her mom called from the sidewalk. "It doesn't look like they're home."

Door after door, Charlie knocked, but no one answered. How was she ever going to sell any cookies?

Just as she was about to give up, Charlie saw a minivan pull up in a nearby driveway and a bunch of kids jump out. Perfect!

Charlie took a deep breath and headed over to their mom. "Excuse me," she said. "I'm selling some cookies I made if you're interested in buying some."

"Oh hello," said the mom. "We just got back from soccer practice, but what kind of cookies are they?"

"Chocolate chip and nuts," Charlie said proudly. "My favorite!"

"Oh, I'm sorry," said the mom. "My youngest is allergic to nuts, so I won't be able to buy any, but I'm sure they're yummy. Thanks for asking."

Charlie hung her head as she walked back to her parents.

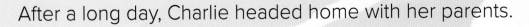

After a long day, Charlie headed home with her parents.

"I'm no good at sales," she said.

"It was your first time, Charlie," said her mom. "We can only go up from here. What do you think you can do so you have better luck tomorrow?"

"Well," began Charlie, "I was nervous every time I knocked on a door. Then when it opened, I couldn't seem to get my words out right."

"Maybe you should practice what you're going to say," suggested her dad. "Every successful salesperson practices what they're going to say and how they're going to say it. That's how you grab your customer's attention. We can practice right now if you want! I'll be the customer."

By the time Charlie and her parents made it home, Charlie had her pitch down pat. But that wasn't the only thing she needed to work on. They carried on their discussion about the day at dinnertime.

"No one was home when I knocked on their doors," said Charlie. "I can't sell cookies if no one's home to buy them. Maybe it just wasn't the right time."

"Well, the last mom you spoke to mentioned soccer practice, remember?" said Charlie's mom. "Also, we went out before dinner so I'm guessing a lot of people weren't ready for dessert yet."

"Do you think we can go after soccer practice ends tomorrow and right after dinner?" asked Charlie.

"Yes, that's a good idea. We should be sure to let the families settle in before you talk to them too. That mom looked a little busy!" said Charlie's mom.

"Can you think of anything else you could do differently?" asked Charlie's dad. "What about that little boy?"

"I was sad he couldn't eat my cookies," said Charlie. "I thought everyone liked nuts."

"A lot of people like nuts, sweetie," said Charlie's dad, "but he has a food allergy so he couldn't eat them."

Charlie thought about what she could do. "Can you help me make a nut-free batch of cookies tonight? I want everyone to be able to eat my cookies."

"Definitely," said Charlie's mom. "Let's clear these dishes and get to work!"

Charlie was excited to get back out there the next day. She packed up her cookies and checked the time before heading out the door.

When Charlie knocked on the first door, she smiled confidently as she waited for it to open. When it did, she was ready.

"Hello, my name is Charlie and I was wondering if you'd be interested in buying some of my delicious homemade cookies. They're chocolate chip cookies and I have some with or without nuts. And they're only $1 a bag!"

The customer was so impressed with Charlie, he bought three bags!

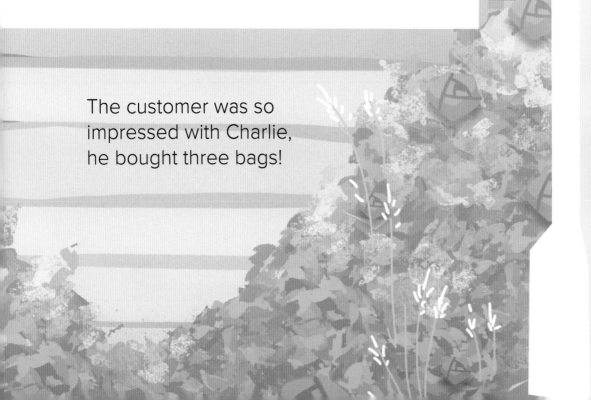

As Charlie continued through the neighborhood, she didn't have any trouble with her customers not being home. Door after door, she sold bag after bag of cookies.

When Charlie saw a familiar van pull up to a familiar house, she smiled wide. After the family got settled, Charlie walked up and knocked on their door.

"Hello, my name is Charlie and I was here yesterday with cookies for sale. I'm sorry your son couldn't eat the ones with nuts in them. I made a whole new batch without nuts," said Charlie, holding up the bag. "And I want to give these to you for him for free."

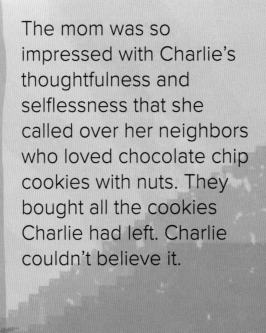

The mom was so impressed with Charlie's thoughtfulness and selflessness that she called over her neighbors who loved chocolate chip cookies with nuts. They bought all the cookies Charlie had left. Charlie couldn't believe it.

At school the next day, Charlie couldn't wait to give her report.

"...And that's how I sold two full batches of cookies and learned all about sales," finished Charlie. "Remember, anyone can be in sales when they grow up—all you have to do is make it happen!"

Charlie's Report on Sales

Important things to know about Sales

1. Believe in what you sell
2. Practice makes perfect
3. Work hard
4. Know who you're selling to and what they like
5. It's not all about making money, it's about helping people
6. Have fun!

I thought sales was going to be boring and something I wouldn't like but it turned out to be a lot of fun. I loved making cookies with my mom and dad and figuring out the best way to share them with people who would enjoy them while making a few dollars along the way. At first things didn't go smoothly but I stuck with it and made it happen which gave me confidence and made me excited to try again! I think more people should consider a career in sales when they grow up so they can make a difference in the world.